The SECRET CIPHER CASES

by Tracey West

Illustrated by Rich Harrington

ISBN 0-439-91448-5
Copyright © 2006 by Scholastic, Inc.

Design by Kim Sonsky
Crime scene illustrations by Yancey Labat

SCHOLASTIC, U-SOLVE-IT! Mysteries club, and associated logos
are trademarks and/or registered trademarks of Scholastic Inc.

12 11 10 9 8 7 6 5 4 3 2 1   6 7 8 9 0/0
Printed in the U.S.A.
First Printing, December 2006

Table of Contents

Itching to Crack a Mystery?

You're in the right place! In this book, you'll find these three mysteries:

 The Hidden Treasure of Hill House:
Twins stumble on clues that claim to lead to a fortune in an old house. Will they solve the clues and find the riches?

CASE #2 **The Secret of the Cipher Society:**
Who is trying to sabotage the school football team? Everyone thinks it's Marcus—and he's got to prove them wrong!

CASE #3 **The Case of the Cat Burglar:**
A jewel thief is sneaking into houses in Amanda's town. Can she follow the clues and catch the criminal?

The best thing about these mysteries is that you get to solve them yourself! Find out what it's like to be a case-cracking detective and see if you can figure out the answer to each mystery. Here's how:

- **Keep track of the clues:** In each mystery, you'll find clues that point to suspects and their motives. Write them down so you can refer back to them when it's time to solve the crime.

- **Study the scenes:** In your kit, you'll also find photos of scenes from each mystery. These photos show important evidence, so study them carefully.

- **Use the decoder:** Each *U-Solve-It! Mysteries* book comes with a set of tools that you can use to solve the crime. In this pack, you'll find a decoder to help you figure out the ciphers in each mystery (a cipher is a code that uses letters or numbers). You'll need your decoder to crack each case!

When you've cracked each *Secret Cipher* case, head to the *U-Solve-It!* web site at **www.scholastic.com/usolveit**. You'll need this password:

CODECRACKED

The Hidden Treasure of Hill House

SATURDAY, OCTOBER 1
3:51 P.M.

Claire Hill sat on her bed and looked out of her bedroom window. Rain pounded against the glass. She didn't have to step outside to know exactly what it would feel like out there: cold, damp, and gloomy.

She sighed. *"Rain, rain, go away . . ."*

". . . come again some other day."

Her twin brother, John, finished the song for her. They had been finishing each other's sentences as long as she could remember. Claire turned around.

"Whatcha doing?" she asked.

"Nothing," John replied, flopping down on the bed like a fish. Even though they were twins, it was hard to tell if you didn't know them. Claire's hair was a little redder than John's sandy hair, and she liked to wear it in two long braids. She was also taller, which annoyed John a great deal, although he didn't talk about it.

"I'm bored," Claire announced.

It wasn't like there wasn't anything to do. There was a game system and a closet full of board games in the family room, and each twin's bedroom had a bookshelf crammed with books. The rain had something to do with their boredom, for sure, but there was something else . . .

"It's the house," Claire said. "I wish we still lived in the old apartment."

"We could be hanging out with Carlos right now, or taking the bus somewhere," John agreed. "I wish we had never moved here."

"Here" was Hill House, which had been in Claire and

John's family for generations. The old, dusty house sat at the end of a long, country road, and the first sign of civilization—a traffic light, gas station, and post office—was more than a mile away.

When the twins' Uncle Harold had left the house to the family in his will, Claire and John's parents had been thrilled.

"Finally, we can leave that cramped apartment," Mrs. Hill had said.

"Think of all the fresh air! We can go fishing every weekend!" Mr. Hill had added.

But the twins missed the apartment and the fact that they could walk a few blocks and buy a soda or take out a library book or hang out with a friend. Their apartment had been small, but cozy, and Hill House, with all its rooms, seemed like a lonely maze.

"And we're the rats," Claire had said. John was normally a little more accepting than his sister—things didn't bother him as much—but today he was in the same gray mood.

"Let's play something," John suggested. "Hide and seek?"

"No," Claire said flatly.

"Pirates?"

"Double no," Claire said. They were both eleven years old now. Pirates didn't sound like that much fun.

John thought. "How about secret agents? We can pretend we're on a mission."

"To find a computer disk," Claire said, catching on. "A disk that evil spies are looking for so they can take over the world. We've got to find it before they do."

"Exactly!" John said, jumping off the bed. "But we've got to be careful. There are spies everywhere."

Claire got off the bed, and John followed her out of the room. Claire was a few minutes older than John, and since then, she usually took the lead, while John followed.

"Where should we look first?" he asked.

Claire nodded down the hallway. "Upstairs."

Hill House was so big that everything the Hill family needed fit on the first floor—three bedrooms, a bathroom, a kitchen, a dining room, a sitting room, and the big room with the fireplace they used as a family room. Claire and John's parents hadn't moved anything upstairs yet, and they ignored the twins' pleas to let them have the second floor to themselves.

"We can save money by not heating those rooms in the winter," Mrs. Hill had said, in her practical way. And that was the end of that.

Claire and John walked down the narrow hallway that led from the back of the house, where their bedrooms were, to the front of the house.

The walls were lined with salmon-colored, pinstriped wallpaper that had probably been very pretty once, but was discolored and peeling with age. Pictures hung on the walls, mostly paintings of flowers, birds, and other things in nature. The dark wood frame above each doorway had been carved with some kind of plant or animal, including butterflies, squirrels, and more birds.

John barely noticed them, but Claire did. If she hadn't been in such a bad mood about moving, she might have found them interesting. But there was a part of her that didn't want to like or accept the house. That would mean that she wasn't upset about moving, and she was.

But the secret agents game was a nice diversion. They marched past the family room, where their parents were scraping wallpaper from the walls, and up the staircase that led to the second floor. They'd only moved in a little more than a week ago, so they hadn't had a chance to explore it yet. The secret agent game gave them the perfect excuse.

The twins walked up the last steps and emerged into darkness. Claire fumbled on the wall, looking for a light switch, and finally found one. A bulb in a glass fixture lit up over their heads, showing three ways they could go: forward, left, or right.

"Our coordinates say the location of the disk is due east," Claire said, nodding toward the right hallway. "But we've got to be careful. The enemy may have gotten there first."

She dramatically tip-toed down the hallway, and her

brother followed. Claire stopped in front of the first door. She put her finger to her lips.

"We have to proceed cautiously," she whispered. John nodded. She slowly turned the doorknob and pushed it.

There was a loud creak. John jumped back. But Claire forged ahead. She flicked the light switch.

They were in a small bedroom, dominated by a big bed with four wood posts. On top of each post was a carved squirrel head. A pale green quilt covered the bed, and fading green wallpaper curled on the walls. There was a dresser, a braided rug, a nightstand, and not much else.

"We've got to sweep the room," Claire said. "Make sure it's clear."

She quickly moved to the closet and opened it, revealing a pole and some hangers.

"All clear," she said.

John started opening up the dresser drawers. "Empty," he announced.

Claire checked the nightstand drawer. "Nothing here," she said. "The computer disk must be in another room."

"Unless the spies already have it!" John cried. "Let's hurry!"

They left the room and tiptoed to the door across the hall. It was locked.

"I left my lock-picking tools back in my other secret agent

outfit," Claire joked. "Let's try the next room."

They crossed the hall again to the next door, cautiously approaching it. This time, Claire let John open the door.

It creaked open to reveal what looked like an office. There was a bookshelf, a stuffed armchair, and a large, wooden desk near the window.

"Maybe the computer disk is hidden in one of the books," John suggested.

Claire nodded. "Good thinking. You check those, and I'll check the desk."

She walked to the old desk, sat in the chair, and pulled open the old drawer in the middle. Like most things in the house, it had long ago been emptied of its contents.

She turned her attention to the drawers on the left side of the desk and opened the top drawer there. She stuck her hand inside. Once again, the drawer was empty.

But as she withdrew her hand, she brushed up against something on the top of the drawer—almost like a knob. She stuck her head as far inside the drawer as she could and looked in.

It was a knob, a small brass one. And it seemed to be connected to some kind of panel.

"It's a hidden panel!" she exclaimed.

"Good job, Agent Hill," John said. "Have you found the computer disk?"

"No, I'm serious, it's for real!" Claire told him. She carefully slid the panel open. An envelope slid out into the bottom of the drawer. Claire picked it up.

The envelope was slightly yellowed, and the writing on it was in old-fashioned script. It read "For Someone Worthy."

John peered over her shoulder. "What's that mean?"

"It's like, for someone who deserves to open it," Claire guessed. "And since we found it, that means us!"

John grabbed a silver letter opener from a cup on top of the desk.

"Here, use this!" he said.

Claire took the letter opener and carefully sliced open the envelope. Inside was a folded-up piece of paper—and something even more interesting. She pulled out a cardboard circle—actually, two cardboard circles, but they had been attached together, one on top of the other. Written all around the top circle was the alphabet, from A-Z. There was a window cut out in the circle, with the letter "P" showing through it. Claire looked at it curiously.

"Hey, I think it's supposed to move. Like a wheel," John said. He reached for it, and Claire handed it to him. He gently pushed the top circle, and it spun under his fingers. Now the letter "Q" showed in the window.

"I get it," Claire realized. "When you move the wheel, a new letter appears in the window, and there's a different letter on top. It's one of those code wheel things. For secret codes."

"Cool!" John said. "Do you think it's from a *real* secret agent?"

"Let's find out," Claire replied. She carefully unfolded the piece of paper inside. The message on the paper was written in the same old-fashioned hand as the envelope. Claire read it out loud.

To Whomever Finds This Letter:

I write this letter on the morn of my sixtieth birthday. For the first time in my life, thoughts of my own mortality haunt me. Although I am fit and in good form, my best years are over, and the shadow of death hovers over me, as it does all those who are elderly.

But my greatest fear is not death. It is that, when I die, my brothers will receive my fortune. My own brothers have spent the last years attempting to cheat and torment me. I am ashamed to say it, but they are bad men, all of them. The thought of them enjoying my fortune when I am gone saddens me.

But I vow that they shall never have it. I have hidden the fortune somewhere in the house, somewhere prying eyes will not find. It is my hope that, years from now, a worthy individual will find this letter, follow the clues I have left, and uncover the fortune. I know that I take a great risk, but my heart knows that even if those with ill intentions were fortunate enough to stumble upon this letter, their dull minds would be inadequate to solve the puzzle. Sadly, all the fortune in the world cannot compensate for ignorance.

So I leave it to you. If you succeed, my fortune will be yours. I only pray that you are worthy and will not use your newfound riches to cause harm to others.

With a sincere heart,
Sebastian Hill
October 1, 1928

GUKPYB HIP XQI NOPJG XBKX HFE, NLX RUAUP GORZ.

Claire and John were silent for a brief moment. Then they both began to speak quickly.

"A fortune! In this—"

"—house! And his name is Sebastian Hill! He has the same last name—"

"— as us! We must be related. But who was trying to—"

"—hurt him? What's an unscrupulous mind? And did you see the—"

"—date on the letter? October 1! That's today! Weird! And what's up with—"

"—those letters at the bottom of the page? It's some kind of—"

"Secret code!" both twins cried at once.

Each twin took a deep breath.

"Do you think it's real?" John asked.

"It looks real," Claire said. "This letter looks old. And if we found the letter, that means nobody else has. So the fortune has got to be here."

John began to move around the code wheel. "I think I know how this works. You move the wheel so that the letter you want to decode is at the bottom. Then the letter on top is the real letter. See? The first letter in the message is 'M,' and the letter at the top of the wheel is 'J.'"

Claire took a pencil from the cup on top of the desk and picked up a small, lined pad next to it. She wrote the letters as John read them out loud. When John finished the last letter, Claire read the message.

"Search for two birds that fly, but never sing."

"That's it?" John asked. "Couldn't it be something like, 'I hid my fortune in the silverware drawer'?"

"It's a clue, remember?" Claire told him. "We've got to find the birds."

"But we can't go outside," John protested. "It's raining."

"But I don't think the birds are outside," his sister pointed out. "These birds fly, but never sing. Maybe they're like, bird statues or something."

"Or paintings," John suggested. "There's paintings of birds and stuff all over this house."

"You're right!" Claire said. "We should go look at the paintings." She stopped, thoughtful.

"I'll hold onto the letter, and you keep the code wheel, all right?" she asked.

"Right," John said, nodding. "That's fair."

The twins practically ran downstairs and back into the house's main hallway, where most of the pictures were. Most of them were too high to reach, but they could see birds in almost all of the paintings.

"I'll get a chair from the kitchen," John said. He ran off and came back seconds later to find Claire under a painting of three blue jays on a tree branch.

"They're not flying, but there's more than one," she said. "We should check it anyway."

"Right," John said. He put the chair under the painting, stood on it, and took the painting off the wall—right as his mother walked into the hall.

"What are you doing?" Mrs. Hill asked.

Claire thought quickly. "We, uh, we're cleaning off the paintings," she lied. "They're really dusty."

Mrs. Hill's eyes narrowed. "What are you using to clean them off? Your shirt?"

"I was just getting paper towels," John chimed in. He set down the painting and dashed off toward the kitchen.

Their mother seemed to believe their story. "I guess you must be really bored to resort to this," she said. "But at least this shows you care about the house."

No, I don't! I never wanted to move here! That would normally have been Claire's reply. But she kept her thoughts inside. She didn't want her mom to get suspicious. Besides, the whole secret fortune thing . . . it definitely made the house more interesting.

John appeared with the paper towels, and Mrs. Hill retreated to the family room. Now that her brother was back, Claire carefully examined the back of the painting. Some faded brown paper was attached to the back of the frame, but there was no writing on it or any other sign that Sebastian Hill had been there.

"I don't think this is it," she said. "But I guess we should clean it off."

John polished the dusty frame, and Claire put it back on the wall. Then they moved the chair underneath the next painting with a bird on it: a robin perched on the edge of a nest of blue eggs.

"That's only one bird," John pointed out.

"I know," Claire said. "But I think we should still check."

John climbed up and retrieved that painting, and Claire cleaned it off. But once again, there was no sign of a clue. They hung the painting up again.

The twins went up and down the hallway, examining every painting that had a bird in it—and every one in between, because Claire had promised their mom that they would be cleaning all the paintings. By the time Claire hung the last painting back on the wall, they were tired—and discouraged.

"Maybe Sebastian Hill was lying," John said. "Maybe he was a practical joker or something."

"Or maybe we're just not looking in the right place," Claire said. "I bet the clue is right under our—" She stopped and stared ahead.

"Noses?" John finished.

Claire pointed in front of her. "Of course! Look!"

From her perch on top of the chair, Claire had a perfect view of the top of the doorframe across the hall. Like all of the other doors in the house, animals had been carved into the wood on the top frame. This doorway—the entrance to the dining room—had two birds in flight carved in it. The birds faced each other on either side of the door, with a flowing ribbon between them.

"Two birds that fly," John said, remembering the letter. "Do you think that's it?"

Claire was too excited to answer. She dragged the chair across the hall. She reached out and touched the bird on the left. The wood felt smooth beneath her fingers. She felt all around the bird, but didn't detect anything unusual.

"Try the other one," John said urgently.

Claire slid the chair over a bit and felt the other bird. This time, the bird's outstretched wing slid under her touch.

"I can move it!" she said. "I bet there's something hidden under here!"

"Is it money?" John asked.

The wing slid upward to reveal a thin depression in the wood behind it. Claire saw an envelope with Sebastian Hill's writing on it. She took it out, slid the wing back into place, and climbed down from the chair.

"Let me open it!" John cried, and Claire knew that was only fair. She watched as her brother carefully tore open the top of the envelope. He pulled out two folded pieces of paper.

"This doesn't look like a fortune," John complained.

"Sebastian's first letter said we would have to follow clues," Claire reminded her brother. "These must be more clues we have to figure out."

John unfolded the first piece of paper, which wasn't a letter, but looked like some kind of map.

"I think it's a map of the house," Claire said, studying it. "Look, there's my bedroom! And there's yours."

"Is there an 'X' on it, like on a treasure map?" John asked.

"I don't think so," Claire said. "Open the other paper."

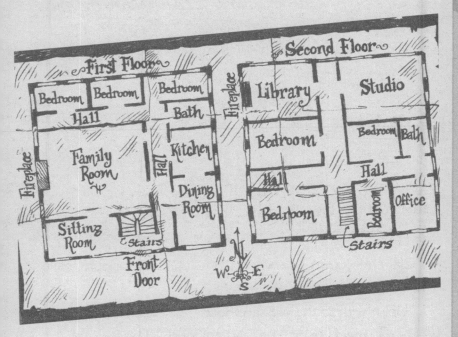

That turned out to be another letter from Sebastian Hill. John read it this time.

If you are reading this letter, then you are diligent indeed, and surely clever as well. I can only hope that you are as kind-hearted as you are keen, for you are one step closer to finding my fortune.

As I write this, I know I have done the right thing, for I have witnessed more bad deeds of my brothers, who see fit to cheat the innocent at every turn. The only one in this family with any goodness in his soul is my brother Caspar's young son Harold, but at five years old he is of no use to me.

With hope,
Sebastian Hill
October 3, 1928

LV. RIPXB XI XBU QUGXUPR JIIP. XBUR GUUT XBU VFKYU QBUPU JKE DUUXG ROZBX.

Claire took the code wheel from John and furiously spun it while he wrote down the letters.

"Up. North to the western door. Then seek the place where day meets night," he read out loud. "This is even harder than the first one. What's all that weird stuff about up and north?"

"I think we need to look at the map," Claire said. "Anyway, did you read that part about the kid named

Harold? I wonder if that's Uncle Harold. He was pretty old when he died—"

"Claire! John! Dinner!" Mr. Hill called out.

Claire folded the letter and map and carefully put them in the pocket of her pants along with the first letter.

"No way! We're about to find the fortune!" John wailed.

"The fortune has been waiting to be found for, like, eighty years," Claire said. "I guess it will have to wait just a little bit longer."

```
SATURDAY, OCTOBER 1
6:00 P.M.
```

Claire and John both agreed without having to speak about it that they would not tell their parents about the Sebastian Hill letters just yet. Right now it was their own secret game, and if they did find the fortune...the surprise would be awesome.

That didn't stop Claire from talking about things, in a roundabout way, while she ate her tuna casserole.

"Did Uncle Harold always live in this house?" she asked out loud.

Her father looked thoughtful. "It's funny you asked. My dad always used to tell me a story about your Uncle Harold and this place. He lived here as a kid, with his mom and dad and some of his uncles. Three of them, I think. From what I

25

understand, the uncles didn't get along at all. Lots of arguments. Then one of them died in a horseback riding accident, and—"

John nearly choked on his casserole, and Claire dropped her fork on her plate with a clatter.

"Sorry!" Mr. Hill said. "I didn't mean to upset you guys."

"That's okay," Claire said. "What happened next?"

"That's the funny part," Mr. Hill answered. "The uncle who died, in his will he stated that he wanted everyone to leave the house until Harold grew up. Then Harold could come back and live in the house."

Claire gave John a knowing look. The five-year-old nephew in Sebastian's letter had to be their Uncle Harold.

"So that guy, the one who died, what was his name?" John asked.

Mr. Hill frowned. "I don't remember. Samuel or Sylvester or something like that."

"Or Sebastian?" John asked.

Their father looked surprised. "You know, I think that's it! Do you guys know something about this house that we don't?"

The twins looked at each other, then gave their father an innocent look.

"No," they said at once.

They continued eating in silence. When they were finished, Mrs. Hill spoke.

"I hope you don't mind if we keep working on the family

room after dinner," she said. "We're getting a lot done. If it weren't for those squirrels—"

"The big stone squirrels?" Claire asked. Two of them flanked the fireplace in the family room. Claire liked them, but her mother had hated them from the start.

Mrs. Hill shook her head. "They're so heavy! I almost think they're bolted to the floor. I can't wait to get rid of them."

"John and I are going to keep on, uh, dusting," Claire said. "Right, John?"

Her brother nodded.

Mr. Hill smiled. "It's nice to see you two hard at work. Good for you!"

As soon as the twins helped clear the dinner dishes, they ran to Claire's room.

"That must have been Sebastian who died in the horseback riding accident," Claire said. "It's weird. It's like—"

"—he knew he was going to die," John said solemnly.

Claire took the letter from her pocket. "That's why we've got to find this fortune. Not just for us, but for him," she said. "Here's what I've been thinking. We found the clue downstairs. So 'up' must mean to go upstairs. If we walk down the hall to the north, the door on the west is the library. See?" She pointed to the map.

"Let's go! We can figure out the day and night stuff when we get there!" John cried.

The twins hurried upstairs and found the library door unlocked. When they walked inside the room, they found two stuffed chairs, shelves and shelves of books, and a fireplace with stone tiles. The tiles were carved with more symbols of nature: a sun, moon, clouds, and lightning bolts.

"Where day meets night," John repeated the clue. "Where's that? A window?"

"Maybe, but that's more like, 'when in meets out'." Claire said. "I was thinking that maybe it's the title of a book."

"I'll check the windows anyway," John said. He ran to the window to the left of the fireplace, and Claire began to search the bookshelves.

As Claire scanned the titles, she realized that searching for a book called *A Place Where Day Meets Night* might be harder than she imagined. The books didn't seem to be arranged in any kind of order, first of all. And many of them looked pretty new. If Sebastian Hill had hidden the clue in a book, he risked that someone might get rid of the book some day. It probably wasn't a good hiding place.

"Maybe it's not in a book," she said out loud.

"And I can't find anything in the windows," John said.

They were silent for a moment.

"Where does day meet night?" Claire wondered out loud. She turned around the room, slowly, but all she saw were rows of books and more books.

"Could day and night be like, a sun and a moon?" John

asked behind her.

"A sun and a moon? I guess so. But why—" Claire turned around and stopped. Her brother stood by the fireplace, staring at the carved tiles. She ran next to him. He already had his hand on a thick tile carved with an image of a sun and a moon overlapping each other.

"Where day meets night—where the sun meets the moon. That must be it!" Claire cried. "Try to move it."

John pressed on the tile, then jiggled it a little. It moved under his touch. He slowly slid it aside . . .

An envelope rested in a small hollow behind the tile. John gingerly took it out and handed it to his sister.

"Your turn," he said.

Claire nodded and opened the envelope. She took out the page inside.

Hurrah for you, I suppose, for if you have come this far, my fortune is now in your grasp. I realize that I must have complete faith that whomever finds this is worthy of the fortune. It is my only recourse. I could put my wealth in a bank and leave it all to dear young Harold, but I fear my brothers would have their lawyers descend and they would retrieve my fortune after all. I can only hope that Harold will come into possession of this house, as my will allows, and find the fortune for himself.

The only pleasure I receive in these dark days is feeding the squirrels and riding my horse, Lightning. On Lightning's back I truly feel free and at peace, but it flees when I return to this dark place.

With a heavy heart,
Sebastian Hill
October 7, 1928

JLU UKGX. HORJ XBU VFKYU XBKX OG RIX IP XBOG XKOF QOFF URJ.

"His horse . . ." Claire said sadly, her voice trailing.

"I know," John said. "It's not fair. He seems like a good guy."

The twins used the wheel to decode the message, and their mood shifted from sad to confused.

"Due east. Find the place that is not or this tail will end," Claire read.

"Okay, this makes even less sense than the last one," John complained.

"Yeah," Claire agreed. "But I think part of it's easy. Due east."

She pointed to the map. "We just have to walk across the hallway."

John nodded. "Let's go."

As far as Claire knew, she had never been in the room across from the library before. When they opened the door, she was surprised to see it was some kind of studio. The north and east walls were filled with large windows that reached almost from the floor to the ceiling; in the daytime, the room must have been quite bright, Claire guessed.

The northeast corner was a solid wall that cut across the corner of the room. A dusty iron sculpture of a squirrel was attached to the wall, its tail sticking out, as though waiting for a hat to be hung on it. Paintings of chipmunks flanked both sides of the squirrel.

On the south and west facing walls were more paintings of animals and birds. A large table in the southwest corner was the only furniture left in the room.

"Find the place that is not," John repeated from the letter. "The place that is not *what*?"

"I don't know," Claire said thoughtfully. "Maybe he made a mistake and left out a word. See, he spelled *tail* wrong."

John looked around. "There's not much in here except paintings." He walked over to the two chipmunk paintings and took one off the wall.

"Nothing," he said after a minute. "Except look. This

painting is signed *SH*. Maybe that means—"

"Sebastian Hill!" Claire finished for him. "Cool. I wonder if he painted all of the paintings in this house?"

"Maybe," John said, "The other painting is signed *SH*, too."

Claire sat on the floor and spread the letter and the map out in front of her.

"I think Sebastian might have made a mistake, except that he had to be smart to think all of this up," she said thoughtfully. She stared at the map, then she looked around the room, sighing.

"I don't think the clue is in the paintings," she said. "I think Sebastian was careful not to put the clues in stuff that might get moved around. That's why the first two clues were hidden in parts of the house."

"But there's no fireplace or carvings in here, just walls," John pointed out.

Claire's eyes widened. "Walls. Maybe . . ." She looked at the map once again. Then she jumped up and ran to her brother.

"See this corner of the room? On the map, the room only has four walls. But this wall with the chipmunks on it is like an extra little wall that covers up the corner. Maybe—"

"—it's covering up something!" John said excitedly. "A place that is not—not on the map! Because nobody knows it's there!"

Claire knocked on the wall. A hollow sound echoed back at her. "You could be right. But how do we get in?"

"Maybe there's a clue in the rest of the message," John suggested. "Remember? 'Or this tale will end.' It must have something to do with a story."

"But he spelled it T-A-I-L, remember?" Claire said. She looked at the wall. The iron tail of the squirrel seemed to be waving at her. Claire reached out and touched it. She tried to move it. Nothing happened at first. But then she felt it budge.

"John, help me!"

John reached up and grabbed the squirrel tail along with his sister. It moved some more. They gave another push and the tail loosened up, turning completely upside down.

That's when the wall began to move.

"Whoa!" John cried.

The entire little wall pushed in, as though it were some kind of door. The twins peered into the black space behind it.

"Do you see anything?" John asked.

"It looks like a ladder," Claire said. "This is some kind of—"

"—secret passageway!" The twins finished together.

"It looks dark," John said.

"I know, but the clue's got to be down there somewhere," Claire pointed out.

"Rock paper scissors to see who goes second," John suggested.

"Sure," Claire agreed. She always won, because John always chose rock, and never seemed to remember that paper beat it.

A few seconds later John was heading down the ladder.

"Hey, come down!" he cried. "There's room!"

Claire followed. The ladder felt shaky under her feet but it held steady. Her eyes slowly adjusted to the darkness at the bottom. She felt a flat wall in front of her. John thrust an envelope into her hands.

"It was attached to the wall here," he told her. I think there's a door here, like a panel."

Claire tried to picture the map in her mind. "Hey, this is Mom and Dad's room!" she whispered. "I bet this leads into their closet."

"Then maybe we'd better get back up, in case they find us," John suggested.

Claire was happy to get out of the dark passageway. She climbed up the ladder and waited for John.

Together they pushed the wall back into place. Then they sat on the floor. Claire handed the letter to her brother and he opened it.

Congratulations! You have found the final clue. If you succeed in deciphering the message, you will soon have your hands on my fortune. I pray, no, I plead, that you use the funds for good. Take care of this house, and of the dear creatures that live around it. And if he is still alive, please take care of Lightning.

It is with a lighter heart that I go for a horseback ride this afternoon. For no matter what happens now, my fortune, for the time, will be safe from those who do not deserve it.

Be well and be wise,
Sebastian Hill
October 8, 1928

JIQR XI XBU FKPZUGX QUGXUPR QKFF. GUUT
XBU YILGORG IH YFLU XBPUU XI HORJ DE
HIPXLRU.

"I wonder if that was his last horseback ride ever?"
Claire mused.

"I don't know," John said. "It's sad. But I know what will
make things right."

Claire held up the code wheel. "Let's do it."

The twins deciphered the message. They read it. Then
they looked at each other.

"Let's tell Mom and Dad!" they said at once.

Claire and John knew exactly where Sebastian's fortune
was hidden.

*Do you know where Sebastian Hill hid his fortune? Use your
code wheel to decipher his last message. Then use the map on
page 23 and clues in the story to figure out the location of the
treasure. Then head over to the* U-Solve-It! *web site at*
www.scholastic.com/usolveit *to see if you're right!*

You'll need this book's password:

CODECRACKED

The Secret of the Cipher Society

> **MONDAY, SEPTEMBER 15**
> **3:05 P.M.**

Marcus Josephs stared out of the library window. Kids walked through the school courtyard, laughing and talking. Kids going home. Going to hang out with friends.

Going to football practice.

Marcus angrily kicked the leg of the table he was sitting at and frowned. *He* should be going to football practice. Instead, he was stuck sitting in detention for no reason. It wasn't fair.

He'd been in the wrong place at the wrong time. Pete Lindstrom and Liam O'Donnel, two guys on his team, had been goofing around in the hallway, shoving each other and laughing. Liam shoved Pete into Marcus, Marcus had slammed into a locker, and Liam took off. And that's when the principal, Mr. Morris, had walked by.

So…detention for Pete and Marcus, and Liam got away clean. And Marcus hadn't even done anything. He sank down

37

in his seat, crossed his arms in front of him, and scowled.

Detention was always held in the library in the back of the school. Mrs. Goodfriend, the librarian, was busy shelving books, not paying much attention to her charges. Each of the kids in detention sat at a different library table.

Pete sat at the table front of Marcus. He had his cell phone on his lap and was sending text messages from under the table. Marcus saw Pete's blonde head bob up and down, laughing. It only made Marcus more miserable.

It's almost like he doesn't care about missing practice, Marcus thought.

At the table next to Pete was Leanne Wells, a cheerleader. She had a cell phone hidden under the table, too, and Marcus knew right away who she must be talking to. Every time Pete laughed, Leanne giggled quietly, covering her mouth with her hand.

At the table to Marcus's right was Brendan Rianni, a kid in the school marching band. Marcus only knew that because he saw him in his uniform sometimes. As a football player, he didn't pay much attention to the band kids. Brendan was there for starting a food fight in the cafeteria at lunch time. Now Brendan was dozing, his head down on the table.

Bored, Marcus turned around to see the last person in the room, a dark-haired girl who sat behind him. Sabrina Athenos was pretty much the smartest girl in seventh grade. She was reading a really thick book right now. Marcus wondered what she had done to end up in detention.

Marcus was in too much of a bad mood to read or joke around, so he turned back around and stared into space, falling into a funk. After what seemed like an eternity, Mrs. Goodfriend walked up and told them their detention was over.

Marcus looked up at the clock: 4:30. If he hurried, he could get suited up and make it to the last half of practice. He bolted from his seat and ran out the door.

TUESDAY, SEPTEMBER 16
9:25 A.M.

Marcus was still in a bad mood the next morning. After

detention the day before, he had arrived at the football field with time still left to practice, but Coach Keebler had sent him home.

"You're late—you lose," the coach had snapped. "Stay out of trouble if you want to stay on my team."

Marcus's mood only got worse when one of the office secretaries came into his science class and handed a note to his teacher. Ms. Merker read the note and then looked up at Marcus.

"Marcus, Principal Morris wants to see you in his office," she announced.

A low cry of "oooooooh" rose up from his classmates as Marcus hurried out of the room, avoiding their eyes.

What now? he wondered.

When he entered the principal's office he saw a familiar group there: Pete, Leanne, Brendan, and Sabrina, his detention partners from the night before. Principal Morris sat at his desk, his balding head shining under the fluorescent office light.

"Some of you may be wondering why you're here," the principal began. "But I expect others of you already know. This morning, one of our custodians made a startling discovery. The statue of Brad Simpson has been vandalized."

"Brad who?" Pete asked.

"The founder of our school football program, of course,"

Principal Morris answered. "It stands in the courtyard outside the library."

Marcus knew that statue—some guy in a suit and an old-fashioned hat, holding a football. He had never paid much attention to it.

Principal Morris stood up. He began to pace back and forth behind his desk.

"Somebody saw fit to paint a mustache on Brad Simpson," he said. Leanne giggled. The principal turned dramatically on his heel and faced them. "And I think it was one of you!"

"No way!" Marcus protested. This couldn't be good.

"The courtyard is locked every day at 4 p.m.," Principal Morris continued, doing his best impression of a TV detective. "The only access is from inside the school, through the library doors. And you all were in the library until 4:30 p.m. One of you must be the guilty party."

Marcus looked at the others. Pete had his usual blank look on his face. Leanne was twirling her long hair around a finger. Brad was yawning. And Sabrina's expression was serious and thoughtful.

But no one confessed.

"Let's make this easy," the principal said. "Just tell me who did it, and only the guilty party will be punished. Otherwise, every single one of you has detention until the culprit is found."

"But that's not fair!" Marcus cried. "I shouldn't even have been there in the first place. I can't miss football practice again!"

"Then perhaps you can convince one of your friends to tell the truth," Principal Morris said. He looked at the group expectantly, but still no one spoke up.

"Very well," he said, sitting down again. "Detention. Until one of you comes clean."

```
TUESDAY, SEPTEMBER 16
11:55 A.M.
```

A dark cloud hovered over Marcus's mood all morning. One day of unfair detention was bad enough, and now there was no end in sight. Coach Keebler would probably cut him from the team.

At lunch time, he sat at his usual table with Pete, Liam, and some other guys from the team. They were all laughing and joking, but Marcus didn't join in. He stabbed at his macaroni and meat sauce with his fork.

Then he felt a tap on his shoulder.

"Can I talk to you?" It was Sabrina.

"Whoaaaaaaa!" Pete and Liam chanted. Marcus tried to ignore them.

"Sure," he said. "What's up?"

"Maybe over there," Sabrina said, nodding toward an empty table nearby.

Marcus nodded and followed Sabrina to the table. They sat down and Sabrina faced him. Her eyes looked deep green, the same color as her sweater.

"I need to talk to you," she began.

"Yeah, I kind of figured that out," Marcus replied.

"See, I know you didn't vandalize that statue," Sabrina said. Marcus stopped slouching.

She had gotten his attention.

"I was watching everybody yesterday. Pete, Leanne, and Brendan all got up to get a drink or use the bathroom—or so they said. But you didn't move the whole time. So I know it wasn't you," she explained.

"So why didn't you tell that to Principal Morris?" Marcus asked.

Sabrina raised an eyebrow. "You think he would believe me? He's not going to give up until somebody confesses. And I don't think we can get anyone to confess—unless we can find proof that they did it."

Marcus studied Sabrina. He didn't know her all that well. They had been square dance partners on Western Day in third grade, but that was about it. She mostly kept to herself. And now she was asking him to do something a little crazy— play detective? He wasn't sure how to answer. Then again, Sabrina was definitely one of the smartest kids around.

"So, how do we find out?" Marcus answered.

"There's still fifteen minutes left in lunch," she said. "I think we should go out and look at the statue. See if we can find any clues."

Marcus thought for a minute. If people saw him sneaking around with Sabrina, he'd probably take some heat for it, especially from the guys on the team. But he wouldn't be on the team at all anymore if Principal Morris kept him in detention.

"Okay," he said finally. "Let's go."

> TUESDAY, SEPTEMBER 16
> 12:15 P.M.

It was a sunny September day, and kids were allowed outside during lunch when the weather was nice. Marcus and

Sabrina walked into the courtyard. A few kids were standing in front of the statue, looking up at the painted-on mustache. A low fence circled the statue, and some flowers had been planted around it.

"So what are we looking for?" Marcus asked, as they approached the statue.

"Something that doesn't belong," Sabrina said thoughtfully.

Marcus watched as Sabrina stepped over the fence and carefully and slowly circled the statue. She had almost completed a circle around it when she stopped and bent down to pick something up. Marcus walked up to her, but stayed on his side of the fence.

"What is it?" he asked.

Sabrina held up a chewed-up pencil. Marcus frowned.

"So? Anybody could have dropped that," he pointed out.

"Maybe," Sabrina agreed. "But most people stand outside the fence. And this was pretty close to the base of the statue." She pointedly put the pencil in her pocket.

Marcus sighed. This was feeling like a waste of time. Sabrina crouched down and was examining the statue carefully. Marcus began to walk around the fence, trying to look like he was helping.

What's the point? he wondered. *What can we find that will do—"*

Marcus stopped. Something white was sticking out of a yellow flower. It looked like some kind of note. He picked it up, and then he walked back to Sabrina.

"I found something," he said.

Sabrina hopped over the fence. "Hey, let me see!"

Marcus looked at the note. On the front were the words "The Cipher Society." He unfolded the paper to find that a message had been written on it in pen, but it didn't make any sense.

ALLC LEAR ATFO UROC LOCK. NEXT MESS AGEL OCKE R5IX.

"It's a cipher," Sabrina said.

"Like the Cipher Society," Marcus realized. "So what's a cipher?"

"It's a message written in a secret code," Sabrina explained. She studied the paper. "This is one of the easiest ones. The message is broken up into groups of four letters each. Turn around."

Marcus turned his back to her. Sabrina took a pen from her back pocket and held the note against his back. He felt her scribbling on the note for a few seconds. Then she finished.

"Okay, look now," she said.

Sabrina had made marks to separate the word groups into their original words. Now Marcus could read the original message.

ALL CLEAR AT FOUR O'CLOCK. NEXT MESSAGE
LOCKER 51.

"Cool," Marcus said. "But what about that X on the
end?"

"That's just there to keep the groups of four even,"
Sabrina replied. "A little trick."

Marcus nodded. He wasn't sure what it meant, exactly,
but he had a feeling the note was important.

"I think whoever did this was part of some group called
the Cipher Society," Sabrina said. "And if there's a next
message, that must mean they're planning something else."

"Oh, great," Marcus said. "So will we get blamed for that,
too?"

Then the lunch bell rang. Sabrina quickly slipped the note
in her pocket, along with the chewed-up pencil.

"See you at detention!" she said. Then she ran off.

```
TUESDAY, SEPTEMBER 16
2:55 P.M.
```

Mrs. Goodfriend must have been scolded for not keeping
an eye on the kids in detention, because that afternoon she
sat at the librarian's desk, and it didn't look like she was going
anywhere.

Marcus took the same seat as yesterday. So did Pete,

Leanne, and Brendan, who was napping again.

"Brendan, aren't you getting enough sleep at night?" Mrs. Goodfriend asked him.

"Huh?" Brendan asked groggily. He lifted his head from his desk. "Uh, sleep. Not really. The band doesn't get the practice field until pretty late. The sports teams get the best times."

"We should," Pete said. "The teams deserve the best. That's who everyone's coming to see, anyway. Not the dumb band."

Brendan's face turned red, and Mrs. Goodfriend frowned. "That's enough, Pete," she warned. "Brendan, I thought the band members petitioned to have the practice time changed?"

"We did," Brendan answered. "But nobody cares about us. Pete's right."

Then Sabrina came running in, two minutes late.

The librarian shook her head. "Isn't being late for class the reason you're here in the first place, Sabrina?" she asked, but her voice was warm. Marcus knew Sabrina was one of her favorite students.

"Sorry," Sabrina said quickly. "Mrs. Goodfriend, can Marcus and I study for our Social Studies test together today?"

Mrs. Goodfriend hesitated for a moment, and then nodded. "Of course," she said. "You might as well make good use of your time here."

Sabrina smiled. "Thanks!"

She slipped into the seat next to Marcus. She took her Social Studies book and propped it up in front of them, partly blocking them from Mrs. Goodfriend's view.

Then Sabrina took a small notebook out of her backpack and placed it on the table in front of them. Marcus saw that she had written "The Cipher Society?" on the front of the notebook. She flipped through the pages.

"I did a little research," she whispered. "I figure that whoever's in the Cipher Society must be interested in secret codes. So I checked to see who's taken out books on codes so far this year."

She showed Marcus the names she had written on her pad: Pete Lindstrom and Melissa Lee.

"No way!" Marcus said, a little louder than he meant to.

"Marcus, Sabrina, study quietly!" Mrs. Goodfriend warned.

Marcus took a pen and notebook from his backpack.

So did Pete do it? he wrote.

Maybe, Sabrina wrote back. *He's definitely our most likely suspect so far.*

Marcus lowered the Social Studies book and looked over at Pete. With Mrs. Goodfriend watching, he couldn't go on his cell phone, so he sat, bored, chewing on his pencil. Something clicked in Marcus's mind.

Pete is chewing his pencil!!!!! he wrote.

Sabrina looked at Pete. Then her green eyes looked keenly at the others.

So is Brendan, she wrote back.

Marcus checked. Sabrina was right. But knowing that Pete was a pencil chewer was all the proof Marcus needed.

Let's talk to Pete after this. Make him confess.

But Sabrina shook her head. *Need more proof. Remember Locker 51?*

Marcus thought back to the note: *next message at locker 51.* He nodded.

Okay. I'll check the locker.

Cool, Sabrina wrote.

Then she closed her little notebook. She took out her Social Studies notebook instead and began to study for real.

Marcus shrugged and did the same. It couldn't hurt to get some extra studying in.

Before he knew it, detention was over.

He stood up and packed up his backpack. He started toward the door, intending to make his way to the hallway that held locker 51. But Mrs. Goodfriend called after him.

"I will be escorting all of you out of the building, so please wait," she said. "We don't want any more incidents."

Marcus gave Sabrina a helpless look.

"I'll check early in the morning," he whispered.

Sabrina winked at him, and for the first time in two days, Marcus's mood lifted. His position on the football team was still in jeopardy, but at least now he was doing something about it. He had a funny feeling Sabrina was going to figure everything out.

Besides, he was kind of having fun.

WEDNESDAY, SEPTEMBER 17
7:50 A.M.

The first class of the day didn't start until 8:00, but Marcus and some of the other athletes in the school were allowed to arrive at 7:15 and work out in the gym. Marcus ran some laps in the gym, and then changed into his school clothes early. It was easy for him to slip out and find locker 51.

Marcus really wasn't expecting to find anything, but to his

surprise, he saw a piece of folded paper sticking out from the locker vents. He looked up and down the hallway. Nobody in sight. He reached up and grabbed the note.

The front looked the same as the first note: The Cipher Society. Inside was another message:

ESAC YHPORT EGASSEM TXEN. EMIT HCNUL RAELC LLA.

Marcus tried to break up the letters into words, like Sabrina had, but it didn't make sense. He knew he had to show this to Sabrina, but he wasn't sure what to do. If he took the note, the person who was supposed to get it would know it was missing.

He quickly took a notebook out of his backpack and wrote down the message. He was just replacing the note in the locker vents when he heard a familiar voice behind him.

"Mr. Josephs, what are you doing in this hallway?" Principal Morris asked.

"Uh, I just finished working out with the football team," he lied.

"Then please join your fellow players until the bell rings," the principal said sternly.

Marcus jogged back toward the gym without another word. He had wanted to hang out by the locker to see who stopped by to pick up the note. He'd have to hurry back once the bell rang.

But at the gym, Coach Keebler spotted Marcus just as the bell rang.

"Josephs, we've got to talk," Keebler barked, and Marcus walked up to him.

"I heard from your friend Lindstrom that you've both still got detention," the coach said. "No practice, no play. You'll be on the bench on Saturday."

"But coach—" Marcus began, but he stopped himself. It was no use. There was only one thing he *could* do—and that was to prove he was innocent. He took a breath. "Fine, coach."

"So straighten up your act, Josephs, all right?" Coach Keebler asked.

Matt nodded and walked away. He went back to locker 51, but the note was gone. He sighed.

He couldn't wait to show Sabrina the cipher at lunch time—maybe she'd figure things out.

Marcus didn't even bother to sit with the other football players at lunch. He grabbed a chicken patty sandwich and fruit cup from the lunch line and took it to Sabrina's table.

"Did you find anything at locker 51?" she asked him.

Marcus nodded. "There was a note. I copied it down."

He took out his notebook and showed Sabrina the message.

ESAC YHPORT EGASSEM TXEN. EMIT HCNUL RAELC LLA.

"I think it's a different kind of cipher," Marcus said. "It's not in groups of four letters, and the letters don't seem to make words when you break them up."

"You're right," Sabrina said. "This is different. It's a backwards cipher."

She picked up a pen and began to write underneath the message.

ALL CLEAR LUNCH TIME. NEXT MESSAGE TROPHY CASE.

"How'd you do that?" Marcus asked.

"Just look at the last letter of the message and read backwards," Sabrina said.

Marcus did, and saw exactly what she was talking about.

"Cool!" he agreed. "So what does that mean? *All clear lunch time*. Do you think something else is going to happen?"

"It looks that way," Sabrina said.

"Then we should keep an eye on Pete, Leanne, and Brendan," Marcus said. "See if they go anywhere, or—"

A wad of chocolate pudding flew past Marcus's face.

"Hey, what the—?"

"FOOD FIGHT!"

Sabrina and Marcus turned around to see kids flinging food everywhere. Chicken patties, buns, bananas, and chocolate pudding seemed to be raining from the ceiling.

"Duck!" Marcus warned, but it was too late. A squished banana landed in Sabrina's hair, and a split second later Marcus's white t-shirt got squirted with ketchup.

"We'd better stay right where we are," Sabrina yelled over the screams that were filling the lunch room. "We don't want anyone to accuse us of starting this."

"You're right!" Marcus called back. "But who do you think *did* start it?"

By now the cafeteria workers and a few teachers had entered the room, trying to restore quiet. One of the cafeteria workers had a girl with long, black hair by the arm and was leading her down the hall, in the direction of the principal's office.

"I guess she started it," Marcus said. "Do you think that's the thing that the Cipher Society planned at lunch time?"

"I guess we'll have to wait and see," Sabrina said.

```
WEDNESDAY, SEPTEMBER 17
2:00 P.M.
```

Marcus and Sabrina learned the truth a little while later, when they were called out of class along with Pete, Leanne, and Brendan once again. Marcus noticed that almost everyone in the school had stains of ketchup and pudding and other food on their clothes; only Leanne and Brendan seemed to have escaped getting hit with flying goo.

Principal Morris looked angrier than ever.

"There has been another incident," he told the group. "The scoreboard on the school field was vandalized. We think it happened during lunch time."

"What happened to it?" Sabrina asked.

"Someone rearranged the letters on the board to spell something unflattering," the principal said. "That's not important. What is important is that there seems to be a pattern here. Our school sports department seems to be under attack."

Marcus noticed that Sabrina raised an eyebrow at this. The principal might have a point. Both the scoreboard and the statue of the football guy were sports related.

"Of course I can't prove who did it," the principal went on. "And with all the chaos at the food fight today, it will be difficult to find the culprit. But I want you to know that I am onto you—and I'll be watching."

Marcus noticed that Principal Morris seemed to look right at him when he said "I'll be watching."

He probably thinks I was up to something in the hallway, Marcus guessed, feeling miserable.

Principal Morris lectured them some more. Marcus's mind drifted, thinking about what had happened. First the statue, then the food fight, and then the scoreboard.

But the scoreboard attack had probably happened during lunch time, Marcus remembered. He thought again about the note: ALL CLEAR LUNCH TIME...

Of course! The food fight had probably been staged to give someone a chance to sneak out of the lunch room and change the letters on the scoreboard. A perfect distraction.

He couldn't wait to tell Sabrina, but Principal Morris made a point of walking the students back to their classrooms. As they walked, Marcus noticed Sabrina carefully eyeing Leanne and Brendan.

"So how'd you guys come out clean after that fight?" she asked casually.

Marcus realized what Sabrina was after. The fact that Leanne and Brendan's clothes were clean could mean that they weren't in the cafeteria during the food fight. She must have figured out what had happened, too, and was trying to get some answers.

"I always keep a change of clothes in my locker," Leanne said. "I wasn't about to walk around with food all over me. Gross."

"Yeah, me, too," Brendan mumbled.

Marcus frowned. He could imagine Leanne having extra clothes in her locker, but Brendan? That seemed odd.

Sabrina looked at Marcus and nodded, as though she knew what he was thinking. Marcus wished they could talk out loud, but they'd just have to wait.

```
WEDNESDAY, SEPTEMBER 17
2:55 P.M.
```

Marcus hoped to walk by the trophy case on his way to detention, to see if there was another message there, but Principal Morris showed up to make sure all of the students got to detention without any vandalism happening along the way. Marcus noticed there was a new member in their group: the girl with long, dark hair who had started the food fight.

Mrs. Goodfriend shook her head when she saw the girl ushered in.

"Melissa Lee, I am so surprised to see you here!" the librarian said. "What on earth were you thinking today,

starting a food fight like that?"

Marcus almost cried out in surprise. Melissa Lee! That was the other kid who took out books about codes and ciphers. He glanced at Sabrina, whose green eyes were wide.

Melissa just shrugged, and a strange smile crossed her face. "I don't know. I guess something just came over me."

"Mrs. Goodfriend, I am sure you will keep a close eye on these students," Principal Morris said sternly. "We don't want any more trouble here."

"I'll do my best, Fred," Mrs. Goodfriend replied.

Melissa sat down at one of the front tables next to Leanne. Sabrina took a seat at Marcus's table again, and the librarian didn't protest.

Marcus noticed that Melissa yawned and closed her eyes, just like Brendan always did.

Must be those late practices, he thought.

Sabrina propped up her science book in front of them, and Marcus took out his notebook. He began to write furiously.

Melissa Lee started the food fight! I think she did it for a distraction. So someone could mess up the scoreboard. I bet she's a member of the Cipher Society.

Exactly, Sabrina wrote back. *And she's in the marching band. Maybe she's in on it with Brendan. He didn't get messed up in the food fight.*

But she's sitting next to Leanne, Marcus pointed out. *And Leanne didn't get messed up from the food fight. Maybe that's because she was outside at the scoreboard.*

But Brendan's reason why he was clean was kind of lame, Sabrina replied.

Don't forget about Pete, Marcus wrote back. *He's a pencil chewer. And he took out those books about codes.*

Marcus wanted to add, "And he doesn't seem to care about missing football practice. Maybe he's got something against the team." But his hand hurt from writing so much.

There's only one way to be sure, Sabrina wrote. *We need to get to the trophy case to intercept the next message, so we can catch them in the act.*

I'll take care of it. Don't worry, Marcus wrote.

Sabrina looked at him and raised her eyebrow as if to say, "How are you going to do that?"

To be honest, Marcus wasn't exactly sure. But he wanted to catch the Cipher Society so badly that he was willing to do anything.

Sabrina had one more thing to write.

I found out what happened to the scoreboard. Someone took the letters from "PINKERTON SCHOOL HORNETS" and used them to spell "SPORTS STINK."

Marcus almost laughed out loud. Even though he was on the football team, it was kind of funny. His laugh came out as a weird little sneeze instead.

"Bless you," Mrs. Goodfriend said.

That gave Marcus an idea.

"Achoo! Achoo! Achoo! Achoo!" he sneezed again, and again, and again.

"Oh dear," Mrs. Goodfriend said. "Marcus, are you all right?"

"It's my allergies," he lied, trying to sound stuffed up. He sneezed again.

Mrs. Goodfriend opened her desk drawer. "Rats! I'm out of tissues."

"Achoo!" Marcus really played it up.

Sabrina joined in. "Mrs. Goodfriend, he really needs a tissue. He's got a snot waterfall working over here."

"Ew!" Leanne cried.

The librarian grimaced. "Okay, get some tissues, but be

quick! Despite what Fred Morris believes, you students are not prisoners here. Just let me get you a hall pass."

She handed Marcus the laminated card, cringing when he reached out his hand to take it. Marcus nodded in thanks and dashed out of the room. He hurried to the front hall of the school, where a large, glass case held sports trophies throughout the years. Principal Morris's office was a few doors down; Marcus could hear his voice booming down the empty hallway. He'd have to be fast.

Marcus looked inside the case, but all he saw were plaques and trophies. He tried to slide open the doors, but they were locked.

Think, Marcus, think. The top of the case was too high to reach. Maybe the bottom…

Marcus ducked down and slid his hand under the bottom of the case. Then he felt something. An envelope. He quickly pulled it out. It was marked "The Cipher Society." Inside the envelope was a grid of letters—and a piece of cardboard with windows cut out of it. The letters on the grid looked like this:

A	T	E	I	C	F
O	R	L	S	L	R
R	E	E	C	P	I
C	U	L	L	E	E
R	P	A	H	C	X
X	A	R	X	B	E

"Oh, great," Marcus groaned. This wasn't like any of the other codes he had seen. How was he supposed to decode this? He stared at the grid. The cardboard was the same size. Maybe…

Marcus put the cardboard on top of the grid. Nine letters showed through the windows. He read them in order, but they didn't make sense. He sighed, frustrated. Mrs. Goodfriend would be missing him.

Then he noticed something. A small magnifying glass in one corner of the cardboard. He turned the cardboard so that the magnifying glass was in the top right corner. Then he looked at the letters in the window.

A-L-L-C-L-E-A-R-B

"All clear," Marcus read out loud. Words! He had found words. And that "B" on the end was probably the start of another word. He gave the cardboard a turn to the right.

From the principal's office, Marcus heard Principal Morris's voice rise.

"I should probably check on those kids in detention..."

Marcus knew he had to hurry. He didn't have a pen and paper, so he'd just have to memorize the message. He quickly turned the cardboard until he read all the letters.

ALL CLEAR BEFORE PRACTICE CIPHERS RULE XXX

Hands shaking, Marcus crammed the wheel and the letter back in the envelope and slid it under the trophy case. He knew the Xs were probably just there to fill up the grid; the message was pretty clear.

Then he saw Principal Morris backing out of his office door as he talked to the school secretary. Marcus quickly ran to the corner and dashed down the hallway back to the library.

"How's your nose, Marcus?" Mrs. Goodfriend asked.

"Better," Marcus said, catching his breath. "I hurried, just like you said."

Principal Morris walked in just as Marcus sat down.

"Everything okay in here?" he asked.

"Everything is just fine," Mrs. Goodfriend replied, and Marcus was glad she didn't mention that she had let him leave the room.

When Principal Morris left, Marcus quickly scribbled a note to Sabrina, explaining what he had found out. Sabrina didn't reply. Instead, she thoughtfully stared at the notebook.

Then she raised her hand. "Mrs. Goodfriend, may I please

look at the school calendar for a moment?"

"Sure, Sabrina," the librarian replied. She shuffled through the papers on her desk to find it. Sabrina walked up and took it back to the table. She pushed it over to Marcus and pointed at one part of it with her pen.

FALL SCHEDULE
Thursday nights

Jr. Football: 3:30–5:30, school field

Jr. Cheerleading: 4:00–5:00, gym

Sr. Cheerleading: 5:00–6:00, gym

Jr. Soccer: 5:30–7:00, school field

Sr. Football: 7:00–9:00, school field

Marching Band: 9:00–10:00, school field

Then Sabrina wrote in Marcus's notebook in big letters: WHICH PRACTICE?

Marcus knew what she meant. The note said things would be all clear before practice. But there were a lot of practices that day. The next event—whatever it might be— could happen at any time.

Marcus never realized that band practice ran so late. Probably the marching band needed to practice their moves on the field, but still, 9:00 seemed kind of unfair.

He brushed the thought aside.

Talk after detention? he wrote.

Sure! Sabrina replied. *By the way, nice move back there.*

Marcus grinned. It *had* been a nice move. Almost as good as throwing a touchdown pass.

```
╔══════════════════════════╗
║ WEDNESDAY, SEPTEMBER 17  ║
║ 4:31 P.M.                ║
╚══════════════════════════╝
```

Marcus walked Sabrina home after detention. They talked about the latest note.

"I don't know what we can do," Sabrina said. "We don't know where the next thing's going to happen, and we can't narrow down the time because we don't know what practice it is."

"And Pete, Leanne, and Brendan all have some kind of practice today," Marcus said. "Although it's probably not Pete, right? Because junior football practice starts right after school, and Pete has detention anyway."

"Right!" Sabrina agreed. "Good thinking. So that leaves Brendan and Leanne, and one of them is working with Melissa Lee."

"Maybe we could hang around the school and see if we see anything suspicious?" Marcus suggested.

"I wish," Sabrina said. "My parents aren't too happy about all my detentions lately. I'm sort of grounded. That's why I want to figure this thing out, fast."

"I know what you mean," Marcus said. He wasn't exactly grounded, but his mom and dad were making him put in extra study time. Besides, he didn't even know where he would stake out. It could be anywhere.

"Let's just see what happens," Sabrina said. "We're gathering evidence. Maybe we'll have enough to expose the Cipher Society after tonight."

"Maybe," Marcus agreed, but he was starting to feel doubtful. If they couldn't prove what was up with the Cipher Society, Morris would probably keep them in detention forever. It felt like he'd never play football again!

> THURSDAY, SEPTEMBER 18
> 8:00 A.M.

The next morning, Marcus didn't have to wait until class started to be called into the principal's office. Principal Morris waited at the front door until he had spotted Marcus, Sabrina, Pete, Leanne, and Brendan.

"My office. Now," he said sternly.

The five students found themselves facing the principal once again. This time, his balding head was bright red.

"Last night, the football equipment shed was vandalized," he said. "Toilet paper everywhere. Shaving cream in cleats. Disgraceful."

Marcus and Sabrina exchanged glances.

"What time last night?" Sabrina asked.

"The shed was fine after junior practice, so Coach Keebler thinks it happened during senior practice. Probably around 8:30, right before practice ended," the principal said with an eyebrow raised, as if he thought they all should know this already.

A light bulb went off in Marcus's head. He knew who had vandalized the equipment shed—and he had an idea why, too.

He looked at Sabrina. From the look on her face, he knew she had figured it out, too.

"Would anyone here like to confess?" Principal Morris asked.

"No," Marcus said. "But Sabrina and I can tell you what happened."

Can you solve *The Secret of the Cipher Society?* Use the clues in the story to figure out who is responsible for the vandalism—and why. Then head over to the U-Solve-It! web site at **www.scholastic.com/usolveit** to see if you're right!

The Case of the Cat Burglar

> **WEDNESDAY, JULY 16**
> **9:45 A.M.**

"**A**manda, can you get me the file on Mayor Mauser, please?" Dan Scarbeck asked.

Eleven-year-old Amanda sighed. "Yes, Dad."

She crossed the small office of the *Bayville Times* to the old gray file cabinet in the corner. When Amanda had agreed to work at her father's newspaper during the summer, she had thought it would be pretty exciting. She imagined herself interviewing interesting people, or going to exciting events with a notebook and tape recorder, taking down facts like a real news reporter. Instead, she spent most of her time filing papers and sending out mail, which was not exciting at all.

"But honey, we do live in Bayville," her dad pointed out, after one of Amanda's complaints. "Nothing much exciting happens here."

Amanda had to admit her father was right. The small town was situated on a bay inland of the Atlantic Ocean. There was exactly one bank, one elementary school, and | one food market to serve the whole town. Bayville was quiet during most of the year, and even the summer didn't get very busy, because most tourists preferred to stay closer to the ocean.

So when the *Bayville Times* came out every Wednesday, it mostly contained news about bake sales and town council meetings and school plays. Mr. Scarbeck wrote most of the articles himself, although he did have one reporter on staff, Andrew Washington, who had been reporting for the paper for years before Amanda's dad owned it.

And then, two weeks ago, the thefts had started.

It didn't seem like a big deal at first. Two families in town had reported some missing jewelry to the police. Chief Harris assumed it was just some kids causing trouble. But then Mrs. Wilson on Shell Street was missing three valuable strands of pearls. When the police investigated, they found a note. It read, simply, "The Cat Burglar."

Now *that* was exciting.

"Dad, let me do a news story investigating the Cat Burglar," Amanda had begged. "I can interview all the people who had jewelry stolen. Maybe there's some connection, like they all have cats or something. And we can ask Chief Harris to let us see the note—"

"Amanda, a 'cat burglar' is just a name for a sneaky thief who breaks into people's houses. It doesn't have anything to do with cats. Don't get carried away," her father said, cutting her off. "That's a job for the police, not reporters of a little weekly newspaper. Chief Harris will take care of this, and then we'll report what happened."

And that was that, and now Amanda was filing again, which she hated. She brushed a lock of curly, brown hair from her face and sighed again. It just wasn't fair.

At exactly ten o'clock, the mail carrier dropped off the mail, as she did every day. Amanda walked to the front desk and took off the rubber band holding the mail together. Sorting the mail wasn't much more fun than filing, but at least it was something different.

Amanda had only been doing it a few weeks, but she already had a system: bills on the left, letters to the editor in the middle, junk mail on the right, letters from the Cat Burglar on the—

"Dad! It's a letter from the Cat Burglar!" Amanda cried. She held the envelope in her hands. It was addressed to the *Bayville Times*, and the upper left corner simply read "The Cat Burglar." All the lettering looked like it had been done with a computer. The postmark over the stamp showed that the letter had been mailed in Bayville.

Her cry woke up Andy Washington, who was dozing at his desk. "There's a cat in here?" he asked.

"No, it's really the Cat Burglar!" Amanda handed the envelope to her father. "Look!"

"Hmmm," Mr. Scarbeck said carefully. "It could be the Cat Burglar, or someone pretending to be the Cat Burglar."

"Come on, open it!" Amanda said impatiently.

Her father slid open the flap and gingerly dropped the contents of the envelope onto the desk. A folded piece of paper slipped out.

Her dad stopped her. "Don't touch it! It could be police evidence."

"But how will we know unless we look at it?" Amanda asked.

Mr. Scarbeck thought for a minute. Then he picked up a pen and used it to open up the folded paper.

"No prints," he explained.

The paper contained a strange note that looked like it had been printed on a computer.

```
    BayvIlle Is borIngs-vIlle! I hope my lIttle
adventures are volumInous enough to make the
news. Of course, If you want to make real
news, fIgure out what I'm goIng to do next.

                         Meow,
                         The Cat Burglar

14-13-26    21-26-3 10-26-9-26-20    8-17-14-8
9-13-26-21-26    14-17-12-26    17-8
16-21-26-8-26-21-1-26-3
```

"It really is the Cat Burglar!" Amanda cried. "And those numbers look like a code." She had received a junior detective kit for her birthday last year and it had a bunch of stuff about codes in it.

"The numbers probably stand for letters," Amanda went on, chattering excitedly. "But how do we figure out which letters? In my detective kit there was this wheel, and you could . . ."

She reached to pick up the letter, but her father stopped her.

"This is a matter for Chief Harris," he said.

```
┌─────────────────────┐
│ WEDNESDAY, JULY 16   │
│ 12:30 P.M.           │
└─────────────────────┘
```

Mr. Scarbeck had insisted on calling Chief Harris. It

seemed like an eternity before he showed up, and then he hinted around about missing his lunch, so Mr. Scarbeck sent Amanda out to get sandwiches. As she walked back to the office, she noticed absently that the wooden letters that spelled out "Bayville Times" over the doorway seemed slightly different. She paused. The "I" in Bayville was crooked.

But that wasn't important now. She hurried in, anxious to see what Chief Harris had to say about the letter. She saw that he had one of his officers dusting the letter for fingerprints.

"Looks clean, sir," the officer said.

"Rats," Chief Harris said, frowning. He took another bite of his ham on rye. "That Cat Burglar's pretty clever. But there's not much we can do without prints."

"Wait!" Amanda cried. "Don't you want to figure out what the message means?"

"You mean those crazy numbers? That's just a bunch of nonsense," the chief said. "Look, the letter 'I' is all wrong anyway. More nonsense."

Amanda looked at the letter again. The letter "I" in the word Bayville seemed to jump out at her.

"Hey, Dad!" she cried. "Come outside! I think I figured something out."

Amanda ran out the door, and her father reluctantly followed. She pointed to the crooked letter "I" above the door.

"I think maybe the Cat Burglar hid something there," she said. "Just look!"

Chief Harris opened the door behind them and frowned. Mr. Scarbeck hesitated, but Amanda gave him the look that usually worked when she wanted to stay up late or eat extra dessert.

"Please, Dad," Amanda said sweetly. "Just check."

"Okay," Mr. Scarbeck sighed. He reached up and pushed on the crooked letter "I". An envelope slid out and fluttered toward the ground. Amanda reached out and grabbed it.

"I'll take that, little lady," Chief Harris said. "Have to check for prints."

Back inside the office Chief Harris opened the envelope and took out a wheel with numbers going all around it.

"It's a code wheel!" Amanda cried. "So we can decode

the message! Can I please do it?"

But Chief Harris insisted on dusting for prints first. When the wheel came up clean, the chief handed the wheel to Amanda.

"Let's see what you can do," he said.

Amanda picked up the code wheel, which was slippery with fingerprint powder. She wrote the letters on a piece of paper as she decoded them:

THE RED JEWEL SITS WHERE TIME IS PRESERVED.

"Well, this is just more nonsense," Chief Harris said. "I'll bet this is just some joker pretending to be the Cat Burglar."

Amanda had to admit that the message didn't sound like it made a lot of sense. Then again . . .

"Couldn't the red jewel be like a ruby or something?" she suggested. "The Cat Burglar likes to steal jewels."

Amanda's dad looked impressed. "You might be right," he said. "But what ruby? And where is it?"

Andy Washington opened his eyes. "There's a nice ruby necklace on display at the Historical Society."

Amanda looked at the message again. "That's got to be it! 'The red jewel sits where time is preserved.' Time is preserved at the historical society, right? I bet the Cat Burglar is going to steal the ruby there."

Chief Harris ate a last bite of sandwich and scratched his chin. "Could be. Maybe we could check it out. The historical society is closed on Wednesdays."

"That's the perfect time to steal the ruby!" Amanda pointed out. "You should hurry!"

"Amanda!" Mr. Scarbeck scolded. "I'm sure Chief Harris knows what to do."

The chief nodded to his officer. "Let's get going." He turned to Amanda and her dad. "Thanks for lunch."

Amanda was glad to see that the chief left the code wheel on the desk. She quietly picked it up and put it in the back pocket of her jeans.

When they had left, Amanda turned to her dad. "Can't we go down to the historical society, too?"

Mr. Scarbeck hesitated. "Well—"

"Come on, Dad! That's what reporters do. We find the news when it happens—we don't sit around and wait for it," Amanda pleaded.

Mr. Scarbeck got a twinkle in his brown eyes. Amanda could see he was getting into it, just like she was.

"Okay," he said. "Let's go."

```
WEDNESDAY, JULY 16
1:25 P.M.
```

When Amanda and her dad arrived at the old Victorian house that was home to the historical society, they saw every police car in town—all three of them—parked in front. Chief

Mystery #1

Mystery #2

Mystery #3

Harris walked down the front steps, frowning.

"That ruby necklace is gone, all right," he said. "Looks like that note was from the Cat Burglar after all."

Tom, the ginger cat that lived at the society, rubbed against the chief's legs and purred. Chief Harris looked down.

"Maybe Tom here's the culprit," he said. "Whoever stole the ruby didn't come through the front door. Looks like they climbed up that elm and got in through the second floor window."

Amanda had taken out her notebook and was busy trying to write down everything the chief said. It wasn't as easy as it looked on TV.

"Can we go inside?" she asked.

"I suppose, considering you're the young lady who figured out that note," he said. "Just stay outside the police tape."

Amanda and her dad walked inside. The front door to the historical society led into a bright room with a wood floor. Glass cases on the walls displayed clothes, household items, and tools from the 1800s, when the town was founded. A pedestal with a glass top sat in the middle of the room. Amanda saw that the glass has been broken. Yellow police tape surrounded the display.

They carefully walked up to the tape. Amanda stood on tip-toes to peer inside the glass case. It was empty, except for a card that read, "Ruby necklace, circa 1854, donated by Mrs. Lillian Welsch."

Amanda slowly walked around the case. Then she spotted something else in there—something that shouldn't have been there.

"Dad, look," she said, pointing. It looked like a piece of torn cloth. She tiptoed a tiny bit closer so she could see it better. The cloth was black, and there was part of a label on it with the letters "Fel" in blue.

The letters looked familiar to Amanda. She searched her mind . . . of course! When she was younger, she had taken gymnastics at the local studio in town. Her mom had bought her practice clothes, and they were all made by the same company: Felix Gym Supply. *But what did gymnastics uniforms have to do with the Cat Burglar?*

"I'll show the chief," her dad said. Amanda nodded, then wrote down "Felix" in her notebook.

An idea was forming in her mind.

```
WEDNESDAY, JULY 16
3:20 P.M.
```

What if the Cat Burglar was a gymnast? That would explain how he—or she—was able to climb up a tree and shimmy through a second floor window. The piece of cloth could have gotten torn by one of the branches, or by a loose nail in the window pane. The postmark on the letter probably meant that the Cat Burglar lived right in town. And the fact that Bayville was a small town might actually help. After all, how many gymnasts could there be?

Quite a few, actually, Amanda discovered. She used one of the office computers to look up all articles about gymnastics that were written in the past few years. Her search had uncovered a few names.

There was Fred Ericson, for one, who owned a private gymnastics studio in town—the same studio where Amanda had taken classes—and all of his students. Then there was Carmela Piazza, who sold real estate in town. Whenever Carmela had been interviewed about real estate in Bayville she always threw in the fact that she had almost made the Olympic gymnastics team.

"When I was training to be an Olympic gymnast, I was an indefatigable competitor," she was quoted in one of the articles. "I am just as persistent when it comes to pleasing my real estate clients."

Amanda took out her reporter's notebook and wrote "Suspects" across the top of a page. Underneath, she wrote:

Fred Ericson
Carmela Piazza
Every gymnastics student in town

The thought of talking to every gymnast in town made Amanda's head spin. Besides, she doubted that a kid—even a high school kid—was a jewel thief who sent coded messages to the police. Most of the kids she knew were too lazy to go to all that trouble.

Amanda looked up at her dad, who was at his computer, busily typing an article about the theft at the historical society. If she told him she wanted to interview suspects in the Cat Burglar case, she knew what he would say. "Leave it to the police."

But maybe there was another way.

"Dad, I'd like to try to write an article for the paper," she said.

"Hmm?" her dad asked. She could tell he was lost in thought.

"An article. About gymnastics in Bayville," she said. "Like, a feature story."

Mr. Scarbeck stopped typing. "Well, that sounds nice, honey," he said. "Go ahead and give it a try. If it's good enough, I'll publish it."

"Thanks, Dad!" Amanda picked up the phone.

She had a Cat Burglar to catch.

THURSDAY, JULY 17
10:15 A.M.

Fred Ericson's Star Studios was just down the street from the newspaper office in the center of town. Fred had been very happy to make an appointment with Amanda for an interview. When she reached the gym, Amanda saw a fancy red sports car parked out in front. She quickly scribbled down the name of the car in her notebook.

When she walked into the gym, she saw a bunch of teenage girls in the room. Some were stretching, and others were working on the balance beams in the center of the room. Fred, a tall, blond man in gray sweats, walked toward Amanda when he saw her, a wide smile on his face.

"Amanda, we miss you!" he said. "You would have been a great gymnast."

Amanda frowned. What she mostly remembered from gymnastics class was falling down a lot and bumping into things.

"I want to be a reporter," she said. "That's why I'm doing this article. On gymnasts in Bayville."

Fred frowned. "You're not going to talk to that horrible Carmela Piazza, are you? If that woman mentions the Olympics one more time…"

"I was planning to talk to her," Amanda said. "She is sort of famous, after all."

"Maybe, but I'm the one who keeps gymnastics alive in this town," Fred bragged. Amanda found she didn't have to ask any questions. He talked and talked about how he loved gymnastics as a kid, and how an injury stopped him from going pro, so he turned to teaching.

Amanda closed her notebook when he was finished. She was about to thank him and leave when she thought of one more question.

"That's a really nice car out there," she said. "Is it yours?"

Fred grinned. "Brand new. She's a beauty, isn't she?"

"She sure is," Amanda agreed. Just then, a girl with long brown hair walked past. Fred put out an arm to stop her.

"Amanda, this is Kat Girard, my top student," he said. "You should interview her for your article."

Amanda noticed that Kat had a small cat embroidered on the right shoulder of her leotard.

"Cute cat," she said.

"Thanks," Kat replied. "With a name like Kat it's a good thing I like cats, right? So what's this about an interview?"

"I'm writing an article on gymnastics for the *Bayville Times*," Amanda explained. "Can I talk to you about it?"

"Sure," Kat replied. "I work at the Cone Zone every

afternoon in the summer. Come by and I'll give you a
free scoop."

"Thanks!" Amanda said, smiling.

Free ice cream was a good reason to smile. But Amanda
was happy for another reason.

A gymnast named Kat who liked cats? She couldn't ask
for a better suspect!

THURSDAY, JULY 17
11:30 A.M.

Even though Kat Girard had moved to the top of
Amanda's suspect list, there was still something bugging her
about Fred. When she got back to the office, she looked up
his car on the Internet. It cost about $75,000.

"Whoa," Amanda said under her breath. That was a lot
of money for a gymnastics coach in a small town.

But maybe not a lot of money for a cat burglar.

THURSDAY, JULY 17
3:00 P.M.

Kat Girard kept her promise and handed Amanda a vanilla
cone when she got to the Cone Zone that afternoon.

"So, what do you want to ask me?" Kat said.

Amanda realized that talking to Kat might not be as easy

as talking to Fred. She took out her notebook.

"Um, why do you want to become a gymnast?" she asked.

Kat shrugged. "My mom wanted me to do it. But it's something to do. Bayville's pretty boring, you know?"

Bayville is boringsville, the Cat Burglar's letter had said. Amanda tried hard not to change the expression on her face.

"So, uh, Fred says you're his best student. Will you be competing any time soon?" she asked.

Kat frowned. "I don't know. My mom's pretty down on me 'cause I'm failing English in school. She's making me go to a tutor. I won't be able to compete in the fall unless I get my grades up."

Amanda asked Kat a few more questions, thanked her for the ice cream, and left.

There was still one more suspect on her list.

FRIDAY, JULY 18
12:00

Carmela Piazza had been so thrilled with Amanda's

interview request that she had invited Amanda to lunch. Her parents had said okay, so Amanda knocked on Carmela's door at exactly noon, her notebook in her hand.

The door was opened by a thin woman whose shiny blonde hair was swept up on top of her head. Carmela wore a sleeveless black dress, and held out a hand with red polished nails to greet Amanda. Amanda noticed that she wore a gold necklace and gold bracelets on both wrists.

"It's about time someone in this town recognized who I am," were the first words out of Carmela's mouth. "Please, come in."

Amanda stepped into the living room, an immaculate space with polished marble floors and leather couches. The coffee table was set with a plate of tiny sandwiches.

"I thought we could eat in here," Carmela said. "It's very comfortable."

"Sure," Amanda replied. She sat down on one of the leather couches and immediately sank into the thick cushions. She shifted around until she was sitting up properly. Then she took out her notebook.

"So, the article I'm doing is about—" Amanda began.

"I was an indefatigable competitor when I was training for the Olympics," Carmela said, interrupting her. Amanda remembered her saying the same thing in the newspaper article she had read. She looked around the room. No books.

Maybe she has one of those word-a-day calendars, Amanda mused.

Like Fred Ericson, Carmela did all the talking, barely giving Amanda a chance to speak. Carmela told a long, dramatic story about how the judges cheated her out of her Olympic spot.

"Those judges robbed me of fame and fortune. It was positively egregious!" Carmela was still fuming twenty minutes later. "And now I'm stuck in this monotonous little town selling real estate."

Amanda pretended to write that down, but she had given up really trying awhile before. Carmela just kept repeating the same bitter story over and over again, using lots of big words that took too long to write down.

Carmela took a breath, and Amanda saw her opportunity and stood up.

"Thanks for lunch," she said. "And thanks for the interview."

"When is the article coming out?" Carmela asked. "Will you be sending a photographer? I will have to get my hair done if that's the case."

"I'll have to ask my dad," Amanda replied. "I'll let you know."

Amanda quickly let herself out the front door.

She definitely likes attention, Amanda mused, as she walked home. *But would she become a jewel thief to get it?*

```
MONDAY, JULY 21
10:00 A.M.
```

The weekend was fairly quiet. The newspaper office was closed, so Amanda worked on her article about gymnastics from the home computer, and spent some time at the beach with her mom and dad. There were no reports of any thefts over the weekend, either.

So Amanda was filing once again Monday morning when the mail arrived. This time, she looked through the pile of letters with a purpose. Would the Cat Burglar strike again?

"It's another letter!" Amanda cried. The return address, once again, simply read, "The Cat Burglar."

Mr. Scarbeck walked up and looked at the letter. "Maybe we'd better call Chief Harris."

"Can't we read it first?" Amanda asked. "There were no fingerprints on the last one. And I still have the code wheel."

Mr. Scarbeck nodded. "All right."

Amanda opened the envelope to find another message.

So you were clever enough to decode my little message. Good for you! But perhaps you won't be so dilatory next time.

                              Meow,
                              The Cat Burglar

14-13-17-8   14-17-12-26,   14-13-26
19-11-14   9-17-20-20   19-11-14-19-13
11   12-24-25-8-26

"What does *dilatory* mean?" Amanda asked.

"I think it means *slow*," Mr. Scarbeck said. "So what about the message?"

Amanda quickly decoded it with the wheel. "This time, the cat will catch a mouse," she read. "A mouse? What does that have to do with jewelry?"

"I'm not sure," Mr. Scarbeck admitted. "Maybe Chief Harris will know. I'll try to get him on the phone."

Andrew Washington looked up from his desk. "Mice like cheese," he said helpfully.

Amanda frowned. That was no help. She sat down at her desk and studied the words. *The cat will catch a mouse.*

The folders she had been filing were in her way, so she pushed them aside. The top folder fell to the floor. She picked it up. The file label read Mauser, Mayor.

Amanda jumped up.

"Dad! I know who the Cat Burglar is targeting next!" she cried.

```
MONDAY, JULY 21
10:30 A.M.
```

Mr. Scarbeck drove Amanda to Mayor Mauser's house, a large home right by the bay. Amanda had taken a guess when she thought the Cat Burglar was targeting the mayor, but "mouse" and Mauser? It made sense. And Mayor Mauser and his wife were pretty rich; they probably had some nice jewels.

When they arrived at the house, they saw Chief Harris and all his officers. Mayor Mauser and his wife stood by the front door, looking very upset. Mrs. Mauser held a little gray cat in her arms.

Chief Harris greeted them. "Looks like the little lady here was right once again," he said, nodding toward Amanda. "Mrs. Mauser kept her diamonds in a safe in the bedroom. The Cat Burglar climbed up to the second floor, pushed the air conditioner in, cracked the safe, and that was it. No more jewels."

Mrs. Mauser was giving a statement to one of the officers. "Ronnie and I always play golf on Monday mornings," she wailed. "But I locked all the doors! I never imagined this would happen. Not in Bayville!"

Amanda wandered over to the side of the  house where a tall tree reached toward one of the side windows. Amanda looked up to see that the window was open. It must be where the Cat Burglar had entered.

Amanda studied the tree. It was an oak, with plenty of thick branches good for climbing. She reached up to touch the first low branch. Then she spotted something.

Amanda gingerly picked it up. It was a blonde hair. She immediately thought of Fred Ericson and Carmela Piazza. *Could this be real evidence?*

With luck, the Cat Burglar would send another message. And maybe next time, they wouldn't be too late.

Amanda was filing folders again that afternoon while her father was on the phone. She couldn't stop thinking about the Cat Burglar. Kat seemed like a strong suspect. She was a gymnast, and she said Bayville was boring, just like the Cat Burglar had said in her first note. But she had *brown* hair. There was no definite proof that the hair on the tree had come from the Cat Burglar, but it seemed likely.

Fred Ericson had that new car. And Carmela—well, Amanda had no real proof against her. But there was something about her Amanda just didn't like. She seemed like a sore loser.

Mr. Scarbeck put down the phone.

"Well, Amanda, your gymnastics article seems to be causing quite a stir," he said. "Carmela Piazza called earlier, asking when we were going to take her picture and if it could be on the front page. And that was Fred Ericson. He kept asking about the article and what exactly you were going to write. He seemed a little nervous, actually."

Amanda thought about this. Carmela seemed anxious to get into the newspaper—just like the Cat Burglar with her clever notes and secret codes. And Fred Ericson seemed like he was hiding something.

Fred's studio was right down the street. She could start with him.

"I'll go talk to Fred," Amanda told her dad. "Be right back."

Fred had a simple explanation for his nervous phone call.

"It's kind of embarrassing," he admitted. "See, I was so busy training for gymnastics that I never finished high school. Most people don't know that, and I started thinking that maybe you would put that in the article, and . . ."

"Don't worry," Amanda said. "That's not important. I won't mention it, okay?"

"Thanks," Fred said, looking relieved. "I don't want to be a bad role model for my students, you know?"

Amanda left the studio feeling more confused than ever. She had a hard time falling asleep that night.

The Cat Burglar could strike again at any time.

The next morning, another envelope from the Cat Burglar arrived. Even Andrew Washington was interested in what it said. He actually got up from his desk to look over

Amanda's shoulder. This time, there was only a coded message.

"This one's kind of long," Amanda said. It read:

```
5-24-25-21     22-11-17-20-25-21-26     14-24
19-11-14-19-13     12-26


17-18     17-12-16-24-7-3-26-21-11-15-20-26.
12-5     9-24-21-2     17-8     11-7     11-21-14!
```

Her father read out loud as she decoded it.

"Let me call Chief Harris," he said. "I just hope this time, we're there before the Cat Burglar is."

Amanda grinned. Suddenly, everything made sense—especially after what she'd just heard from Fred.

"It doesn't matter if we do," she said. "There's a clue in this message. I know who the Cat Burglar is!"

Can you solve The Case of the Cat Burglar? *Use your decoder to decipher the last message. The message, along with clues in the story, will help you figure out the identity of the thief. Then head over to the* U-Solve-It! *web site at* **www.scholastic.com/usolveit** *to see if you're right!*